For Liz, the Strong
—S.C.

To Melissa, with love
—E.U.

I am
Strong

RODALE KiDS

Today is field day.
I wake up early
to get ready.

I lace up
my new sneakers.

Dad makes a big,
healthy breakfast.
I feel strong.

All the students
head to the big field.
Captains get picked.
Teams get picked next.

One by one,
everyone joins their team.

Joe picks me.
I am excited.
I know I can help
the blue team.

I am faster
than I look.
I am strong, too.

First up is
the relay race.
We have five minutes
to warm up.
I know what to do!

8

I show my team
how to pass the baton.

The race starts.
I cheer on my team.

Now it's my turn.
I hold tight, run fast, and pass it carefully.
We finish strong.

We go to our next event.
It is a huge puzzle.
The pieces are bulky.
Everyone is rushing to put
the puzzle together.

I try to help.
I step back and look.
I see the solution.

"It's just like passing the baton," I say.
"Slow down and work together."

We work together.
We finish the puzzle.
We are a strong team.

It is time for
the three-legged race.
Ana and I are partners.

Some people laugh.
They call us "short stuff."
But we are a good match.

Other teams stumble and fall.
Ana and I are in step.
We get faster as we go.

18

Our size is our strength
and we win!

We head to the next event.
It's the water balloon toss.
I know I can do this.

I know it!

I get three tries.
My first shot is too high.
My second one goes
off course.

I take my last shot.
I pull back as far as I can.
Bull's-eye!

It is time for
our last event—
the obstacle course.
Three teams are tied
for first place.

24

My team has a plan.
We will do each obstacle
together as a team.

FINISH

We help each other climb the ropes up and down the wall.

We wait and cheer
as everyone hops
through the hoops.

We go slow and steady
on the wavy beam.

We take the lead
on the ski boards.

The blue team crosses
the finish line together!

Today is a great day!
I helped the team in
every way I could.
I never gave up.
I am strong!

What makes YOU feel strong?

Can you think of three examples?

Also available:

I Am Brave

Look for these other titles in the
POSITIVE POWER series:

- **I Am Thankful**
- **I Am Kind**
- **I Am Smart**
- **I Am Helpful**

To learn more about Rodale Kids Curious Readers,
please visit RodaleKids.com.